ALEX'S OUTING

Mary Dickinson

Pictures by Charlotte Firmin

Hippo Books
Scholastic Publications Ltd.
London

Scholastic Publications Ltd.,
10 Earlham Street, London WC2H 9RX

Scholastic Inc.,
730 Broadway, New York, NY 10003, USA

Scholastic Tab Publications Ltd.,
123 Newkirk Road, Richmond Hill,
Ontario L4C 3G5, Canada

Ashton Scholastic Pty. Ltd.,
PO Box 579, Gosford, New South Wales,
Australia

Ashton Scholastic Ltd.,
165 Marua Road, Panmure, Auckland 6,
New Zealand

First published by Andre Deutsch Limited, 1983

Published in paperback by Scholastic Publications Ltd., 1984
Reprinted 1985, 1986, 1987

Text Copyright © Mary Dickinson
Illustrations copyright © 1983 Charlotte Firmin

ISBN 0 590 70306 4

All rights reserved

Made and printed by Hong Kong by Everbest Printing Co., Ltd.

'We're going to the countree
           the countree
           the countreeeeee,' shouted Alex and
Roy and Bernice and Barnie and Greg and Wendy
as they waited for the bus to come.

'Stop that terrible noise,' said Wendy's
mother. 'Wendy, come and stand with me.'
'I think it's meant to be singing,' said Alex's
mother.
'They're very excited about the outing,' said
Barnie's mother.
Just then the bus arrived.

The mothers sat at the front of the bus.
The children rushed to the back.
There they bounced up and down on the
springy seats all the way to the country.
Wendy had a lovely time.
Her mother kept saying, 'Be quiet.' But
nobody seemed to hear.

'This is where you lot get off,' shouted the driver.

Everyone got off.

All around them the country looked very smooth and green.

It made Alex want to run. Run as fast as he could.

'Beat you to the trees,' he cried, and before the mothers could shout stop, the children were running away.

'They'll get lost,' said Wendy's mother.

'Don't worry,' said Alex's mother. 'They won't go far.'

It wasn't long before Alex stopped.
His tummy hurt and his feet felt very heavy.
Suddenly he felt frightened. He was all alone
in the country.
He tried to turn back, but his feet wouldn't
move.
'Help,' cried Alex. 'I'm stuck in the mud!'

Roy and Greg came and pulled him out.
There was a lot of slipping and splashing
and Alex fell over.
'You're very muddy,' said Wendy. 'I get told
off if I get dirty.
'Well I don't,' said Alex crossly.

'Children," called the mothers, 'come and look at the cow.'
'I don't like cows,' said Alex, and he mooed as loudly as he could at the cow.

The cow didn't move, but there was a
squelchy thundering noise, and a whole herd
of cows came galloping up and breathed
over Alex.
'I think they like you,' said his mother.
'Aren't they big?' said Bernice.
'Oh do be careful, Wendy,' said her mother,
'they might splash you.'
'Come on, it's time to eat,' said Alex's
mother, walking away.
'I'm not hungry,' complained Alex.
But everyone else was.

While the others ate, Alex swung about in the trees.

'Look Mum, look at me,' he shouted. But Alex's mother didn't look. She was too busy talking to Barnie's mother.

There was a ripping sound.

'Oh Alex,' whispered Wendy. 'You've torn your jeans. Bet your mother will be cross.'

'No,' said Alex, 'she didn't see.'

Alex decided it was time he had lunch.
He ate all his lunch and lots of everybody
else's.

After lunch the mothers picked blackberries.
Alex felt too full to eat any, so he put some in
his pocket for later. Then he crept among the
bushes with Roy trying to frighten Wendy.
'Stop it!' said Wendy, throwing blackberries
at Alex. 'You're just stupid and messy.'
'Hee! Hee!' laughed Alex. 'You've got
purple from the blackberries all over you.
Bet your mother will be cross!'
'Oh dear,' said Wendy sadly.

When it was time to go home, Alex sat with his mother.

She was *still* talking to Barnie's mother. In the seat behind, Wendy's mother was wiping Wendy's face and telling her off.

Poor Wendy, thought Alex.

On the way home from the bus stop Alex's
mother showed him the blackberries she had
picked.
Alex remembered the ones in his pocket.
He slid in his hand.
Ugh.
His pocket was all wet and sticky. The
blackberries were very squashed. There was
a big patch of purple on his jeans.
Will Mum be cross, wondered Alex.

When they got home Alex went straight into
the bathroom, took off his clothes and hid
them in the dirty clothes basket.
'What are you up to?' asked his mother.
'I fancy a bath,' said Alex.
Alex's mother looked surprised.
'You usually hate baths. Quick let's get you
in before you change your mind.'

When Alex was in the bath, his mother
found his clothes.
Alex waited. Was she going to be cross?

'What a mess,' said Alex's mother loudly.
But then she looked at Alex and smiled, 'I
suppose I should have guessed. I don't mind; it
was such a lovely outing.'